Mr. Basset Plays

DOMINIC CATALANO

Boyds Mills Press

For Oksana...
just because
—D.C.

Text and illustrations copyright © 2003 by Dominic Catalano
All rights reserved

Published by Boyds Mills Press, Inc.
A Highlights Company
815 Church Street
Honesdale, Pennsylvania 18431
Printed in China
Visit our Web site at www.boydsmillspress.com

Publisher Cataloging-in-Publication Data (U.S.)

Catalano, Dominic.
    Mr. Basset plays / written and illustrated by Dominic Catalano.
—1st ed.
[32] p. : col. Ill. ; cm.
Summary: A wealthy, but unhappy, basset hound searches for what's
missing in his life and discovers what he needs are friends.
ISBN 1-59078-007-8
1. Friendship — Fiction. 2. Dogs — Fiction. I. Title.
  [E] 21 AC CIP 2003
200210579

First edition, 2003
The text of this book is set in 16-point Bernhard Modern.

10 9 8 7 6 5 4 3 2 1

Mr. Reginald E. Basset lived in glorious Hound Hall. He was wealthy beyond anyone's wildest dreams. He bought and sold at his whim anything and everything he desired.

He lived in his mansion surrounded by servants and drivers and cooks. But he lived there all alone.

Early each morning, Walter the butler would enter
Mr. Basset's bedroom and yip, "Up and at 'em, sir. Much to do."

Walter would hand Mr. Basset a list as long as the hind leg
of a greyhound.

"Too much to do," Mr. Basset would say, yawning.

"But all very important, sir," Walter would say. "Contracts to sign,
goods to buy, employees to pay."

"All very important," Mr. Basset would whimper to himself.
But in his heart he felt something was missing.

One day Mr. Basset sat at his desk, which was piled high with important papers.

Absentmindedly, he gazed out the window. He saw a group of children in the park next door. Slowly, a smile curled his lip and then a grin spread wide across his muzzle.

"Walter!" he barked.

When Walter entered the room, Mr. Basset was pacing excitedly.

"Walter, what are those children doing out there?"

"Why, they're playing, sir," said Walter, looking toward the park.

"By my grandmother's tail, I know what I've been missing!" Mr. Basset barked, his own tail wagging. "I want to play!"

"You wish to play, sir?" Walter replied. "Very good, very good indeed, sir."

Mr. Basset looked through his telescope to get a better view.

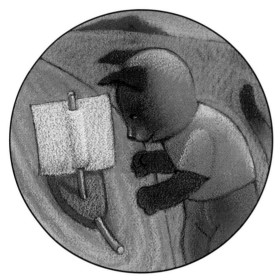

Children were sailing toy
boats in the pond,

painting pictures,

riding toy horses,

and blowing musical
instruments.

"We have much to do!" Mr. Basset barked. "Take down this list, Walter!"

"As you wish, sir," said Walter. Mr. Basset returned to his telescope and dictated the following words, which Walter wrote down in an elegant paw:

Boat
Art
Horse
Music

"These are things I'll need in order to play!" Mr. Basset yapped happily. He looked at the list Walter had written. "Let's go and buy a boat!" said Mr. Basset.

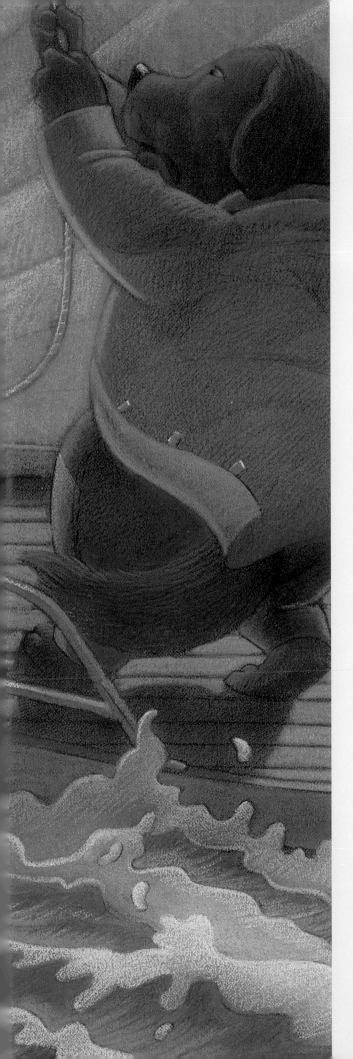

M r. Basset sailed all afternoon on his new sixty-foot yacht. Unfortunately, the lake was a wee bit rough. The yacht didn't seem as much fun as the boats the children sailed on the pond. "Walter," Mr. Basset whined, "playing with boats just isn't for me."

Walter crossed out the first word on Mr. Basset's list.

~~Boat~~
Art
Horse
Music

The following week, Mr. Basset and Walter raced around the world collecting art. It filled the greatest room of Hound Hall.

"Just lovely, sir," said Walter.

While the art moved Mr. Basset's heart, it wasn't the same as what he had seen through his telescope.

"What's next on the list, Walter?" Mr. Basset whimpered.

~~Boat~~

~~Art~~

Horse

Music

H orses were much too big!

"This is not for me!" Mr. Basset growled. His heart sank as he carefully dismounted. "I'll never get to play," he said, blinking back a tear.

"No worries, sir," said Walter. "There's still music!"

~~Boat~~

~~Art~~

~~Horse~~

Music

Ⓑut even a full symphony orchestra filling cavernous Basset Music Hall with glorious sound didn't seem enough.

Something was missing.

~~Boat~~

~~Art~~

~~Horse~~

~~Music~~

Mr. Basset crumpled the list and leaned his head back. His mournful howl silenced even the brass section.

With all his money, he couldn't buy what he truly wanted.

"Well, I guess it's back to work," Mr. Basset whimpered.

"Whatever you wish, sir," said Walter.

But Mr. Basset couldn't work. He padded around Hound Hall for days. He neglected to sign contracts. He didn't bother with business. He forgot to pay his employees. Within a week, he had taken to his bed. His nose was warm and his fur had lost its luster.

"Poor Mr. Basset," said Walter.

W eeks passed. Now it was Walter who gazed out the window. He watched the children playing in the park. His tail wagged as he peered through Mr. Basset's telescope for a closer look.

Suddenly, he raced to Mr. Basset's room.

"It's a beautiful day, sir," Walter said firmly. "I must insist on your getting some sun."

Mr. Basset looked at him blankly, but didn't even have the strength to nip as Walter eased him into a wheelchair.

Walter pushed Mr. Basset through the garden and close to the park wall. They could hear the children playing on the other side. Mr. Basset turned his head away, growling softly.

Then a ball came sailing out of the sky toward Mr. Basset. Without thinking, he raised his paws and caught it right in front of his nose.

"Hey, mister, nice catch! Could you throw it back?" a puppy called.

Mr. Basset pushed himself out of the wheelchair and threw the ball back over the wall. His tongue hung from his mouth as he laughed out loud.

"Nice throw, mister!" shouted a little calico cat. "Hey, you want to play?"

The next morning, Mr. Basset barked for Walter. "Write down the following," he said excitedly.

"As you wish, sir," said Walter, taking out his pad and pen.

"Play with my friends!" said Mr. Basset as he raced out the front door of Hound Hall.

"Come on, Walter," he shouted, "that includes you!"

And play with his friends is
precisely what Mr. Basset did.